World Wide Web
for beginners

Asha Kalbag

Design and DTP by Isaac Quaye and Russell Punter
Illustrations by Andy Griffin
Additional Illustrations by Isaac Quaye

Technical consultant: Liam Devany
Additional consultancy by Lisa Hughes
Edited by Philippa Wingate and Jane Chisholm
Managing Designer: Steve Wright

About this book

The World Wide Web, also called "WWW", or the "Web", is a huge collection of information. This information covers an enormous variety of subjects, from ancient history to the weather, local entertainment to international sport.

The Web is one of the facilities offered by the Internet or the "Net". The Net is a worldwide computer network, which means that it is made up of millions of computers linked together so that they can share information.

Web pages

Each piece of information on the Web is presented as a document that appears on a computer's screen. These documents are called Web pages. There are millions of pages on the Web and they are all linked together. Anyone using the Web can use these links to move from one page to another quickly and easily.

All the pages are stored on computers belonging to all kinds of organizations all over the world. If you connect your computer to the Internet, you will be able to enjoy all the exciting things the Web has to offer. This is known as going "on-line".

Getting connected

World Wide Web for Beginners will tell you how to get connected to the Internet so that you can use the Web. You will find out exactly what hardware and software you need. Once you are ready to explore the Web, this book will tell you how to find interesting things to see and do.

Once your computer is connected to the Net, you can look at Web pages stored on computers all over the world.

A new language

People who use the Web, known as users, have made up lots of weird and wonderful new words. Find out what some of them mean on pages 44 to 46.

Helpful hints

Throughout this book, there are tips on how to use the Web effectively and efficiently. They will tell you how to deal with some of the problems you might come across. On page 42, there is some advice on choosing a company which will give you access to the Net. Page 43 tells you where you can find more information about some of the things covered in this book.

This picture shows some of the organizations which have Web pages, and what they use them for.

Up-to-date information

This book contains a lot of basic information that will enable a new user to learn how to use the Web. The Web, however, is changing rapidly. Information is continually being added and removed, and software manufacturers often make improvements to Web software. The most recent information about the Web and its software is on the Web itself. This book will show you exactly how to find this up-to-date information.

Museums and galleries display pictures of exhibits.

Banks and other businesses advertise their services and products.

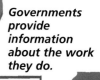

Governments provide information about the work they do.

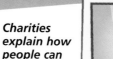

Entertainment companies promote music, games and TV shows.

Charities explain how people can help.

Schools and universities share information and ideas.

Web pages

The information on the Web can be presented in a variety of ways. Web pages may contain words or pictures, or more exciting ways of presenting information, such as video clips. Many Web pages are "multimedia" documents. This means two or more methods of presenting information have been combined in a single page. So a page with both pictures and sounds is an example of multimedia.

This section shows some of the kinds of pages that are on the Web, and some of the ways in which the information is presented.

Video and animation

Some pages contain moving images. For example, you can watch extracts from movies and clips from music videos. Short animation sequences are sometimes added to Web pages to make them more exciting.

Up-to-date information

Web pages can be updated regularly, so they are particularly useful for displaying news, weather forecasts and sports results. Web pages may contain charts and graphs which continually update themselves according to the latest statistics. You can also find travel information, such as train and plane times, on the Web.

Software

There are many Web pages that tell you where to find software on the Internet. A wide variety of programs are available for you to copy onto your computer. Some of them are free, others you have to pay for. Many of the programs help you to enjoy the Web more, by allowing you to watch the videos and listen to the music included on some pages.

Music and sound

Web pages can contain sounds, such as recordings of famous speeches or sound effects. There are Web pages devoted to different types of music, from classical to country, and punk to pop. Some of these pages include music clips to listen to.

Personal pages

Many people create Web pages to share information about themselves or their interests with other Web users. Some personal pages contain photographs of the people who wrote them, their friends and their families.

Pictures

You can find a variety of pictures on the Web. Pictures created using a computer, called computer graphics, photographs, maps and diagrams are often used to illustrate factual information and stories. Some Web pages contain only pictures. You can find photographs of places, wildlife, famous people, and works of art.

Bigger and better

The Web is a very popular part of the Internet. More and more people and organizations are adding their own pages to it every day. As a result, the Web is growing rapidly. The information is frequently updated, and improvements in technology allow people to present it in new and exciting ways.

Getting connected: the hardware

On these pages you can find out exactly what equipment you need to use the Web.

A computer

A multimedia PC

Speakers allow you to hear sounds on Web pages.

A mouse

Web pages appear on your computer screen or "monitor".

You don't need a brand new computer to browse the Web. If you have a PC which has at least a 386 processor chip, you will be able to connect to the Internet. If you are using a Macintosh, your computer needs a 8036 chip or better.

Your computer needs a lot of RAM (Random Access Memory). RAM is the part of your computer's memory which enables it to use programs. Memory is measured in bytes, and 1 megabyte (MB) is just over a million bytes. Your computer needs at least 16MB of RAM to use Internet and Web software (you can find out about this software on pages 8 and 9).

Software, and any other information you want to save permanently, is stored on your computer's hard disk. Your computer needs at least 200MB of free hard disk space to store Net and Web software. (Free space is storage space that isn't being used by other programs.)

A modem

The easiest way to join up your computer to the Net is by using a telephone line.

There are two main ways of sending information across telephone networks. It can be sent either in the form of sound waves, which are called analog signals, or as electronic pulses, which are called digital signals.

A computer produces data in digital form. To communicate over analog telephone lines, it needs a device called a modem. A modem converts digital signals into analog signals and back again.

Ask the company that provides you with a telephone service what kind of telephone lines your telephone uses. If it uses analog lines, you will need a modem.

This picture shows two computers on the Internet exchanging information using modems.

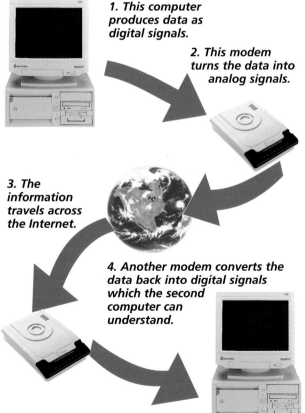

1. This computer produces data as digital signals.

2. This modem turns the data into analog signals.

3. The information travels across the Internet.

4. Another modem converts the data back into digital signals which the second computer can understand.

6

Which modem?

There are two types of modems that can be used with desktop computers: internal modems and external modems.

An internal modem fits inside your computer's processing unit. An external modem sits on your desktop. It has a cable which plugs into one of the sockets in your computer's processing unit. This socket is called a serial port.

Modem speed

Modems transfer data to and from the Net at different speeds. The speed is measured in bits per second (bps). It is best to buy the fastest modem you can afford. Make sure it works at no less than 28,800 bps. If you have a high-speed modem you will spend less time waiting for Web pages to appear on your screen.

A telephone line

You must be able to plug your modem into a telephone point. To do this, you may have to move your computer or use an extension lead.

If you have only one telephone line, you won't be able to receive or make telephone calls while you are connected to the Internet.

Special Internet computers

If you don't already own a computer, and only want one to access the Internet, you may consider buying a Network Computer (NC). These machines are less expensive than ordinary computers because they only allow you to use the Internet. They are not as powerful as ordinary computers and rely on other computers on the Internet to store and process data for them.

Extra hardware

If you want to use the Web for a specific purpose, such as watching video clips or playing games, you may need to add some extra hardware to your computer.

Video To enjoy the animation and videos that are available on the Web, your computer needs a powerful graphics card. If your computer doesn't have the right kind of card, the pictures will be fuzzy and will move slowly.

All Macintoshes and most PCs with Pentium processors contain suitable graphics cards. Otherwise you may need to buy a better card. To watch videos, you need at least a 32 bit card with 2MB of Video RAM (VRAM).

Sound If you want to hear sounds on the Web, your computer must have a sound card. This is a device which enables your computer to produce sound. Macintoshes and multimedia PCs already contain sound cards and speakers. If you have another kind of computer you may need to have these added.

Sound cards

Gaming equipment If you want to play some of the games available on the Web, you will find it easier with a joystick. For games in which you pretend to control a vehicle, a driving wheel. may be useful.

A driving wheel

To use the World Wide Web, you will need to add some special programs to your computer. In this section you will find out what these programs are and how you can obtain them.

Web software

One of the programs you will need is called a browser. This is a program which allows you to look at Web pages.

A browser consists of a window which has two main parts: a central area where Web pages are displayed, and a panel with various buttons and menus which you use to control the browser. (You can find out how to open your browser window on page 11.)

The two most popular browsers currently available are Netscape Navigator and Microsoft® Internet Explorer. Their windows are shown below.

Which browser?

This book explains how to use both Netscape Navigator and Microsoft Internet Explorer to explore the Web. Wherever necessary, there are two sets of instructions for the same activity.

If you have Netscape Navigator, follow the instructions next to this icon.

If you are using Microsoft Internet Explorer, follow the instructions next to this icon.

Don't worry if you have another browser, or a different version of the browsers used here. Most browsers have the same basic functions, so you should be able to work out how to use the one you have quite easily.

The Netscape Navigator window

Menu bar

The tool bar buttons help you to find your way around the Web.

Menu bar

Web pages are displayed in this area.

The Microsoft Internet Explorer window

Browser updates

Companies that make browsers are continually improving their programs. The first browsers available to Net users could only show words and still pictures, but newer versions can handle more complicated methods of showing information, such as moving pictures.

To enjoy new and exciting ways in which information is presented on Web pages, you will need to keep updating your browser. You can use the Web to copy a more recent version of your browser off the Internet onto your computer. (Find out how to copy software off the Net on pages 26 to 29.)

Looking good

Some Web pages have been "optimized" for a particular browser. This means they look and work better when you look at them with that browser.

You can still look at an optimized page with another browser, but you will not be able to see all the decorative features. If there is enough space on your computer's hard disk, you may want to keep more than one browser on your computer, so that you can always see pages at their best.

Internet software

There are other programs that you need in order to use the Internet.

Your computer needs a "dialer". This is a program which enables it to operate your modem and connect to the Net.

You may also need a program which allows your computer to communicate with other Internet computers.

All computers on the Internet use the same language. It is called TCP/IP (Transmission Control Protocol/Internet Protocol). PCs running Windows 95 and Macintoshes running MacOs system 7 or better, are already able to use TCP/IP. If you have other equipment, your computer will need a TCP/IP program.

Obtaining software

Web and Internet software is sometimes given away with Internet magazines. Most people, however, obtain it from an "access provider". This is a company that you pay in order to gain access to the Internet.

An access provider has computers which are permanently linked to the Net. It allows you to connect your computer to one of these. If you make this connection using a telephone line, it is called a "dial-up" connection.

When you open an account with an access provider, they will send you a CD or floppy disks containing a browser and the other software you need to dial up a connection and use the Net. Make sure you tell them what kind of computer you are using so they send you the correct software. (You can find out how to choose an access provider on page 42.)

Installing your software

To install your Internet software, carefully follow the instructions included with it.

A message will appear on your screen telling you if the installation has been successful. If you have any problems, call your access provider's helpline for advice. The telephone number of the helpline should be sent to you with the software.

Your computer must be joined up to the Internet before you can use the Web. If it is not permanently joined up, you will need to dial up a connection to your access provider's computer. These pages will show you how to go on-line.

How to dial up a connection

Open up your connection software. There may be a button or menu item which tells your modem to try to dial up a connection. If there isn't, open your Web browser by double-clicking on its icon.

 This is the Netscape Navigator icon.

 If you have Internet Explorer you will see this icon.

Your browser may automatically instruct your modem to make a connection to the Internet. If not, a message will appear asking you if you want to connect. Click *OK* or *Yes*.

If your access provider has given you a password, a box requesting it will appear at this stage. Type in your password carefully.

What does your modem do?

Your modem sends a signal to your access provider's computer. This signal, known as a handshake, tells the remote computer who you are, and confirms that you have permission to use it to connect to the Net. While this is happening, you may hear some strange squealing sounds from your modem.

Connected

If your dial-up is successful, a message or an icon will tell you that you are connected.

Connected

No connection

Your dial-up may not be successful the first time. This usually happens when a lot of people are trying to go on-line at the same time.

If you are unable to connect, an error message will appear on your screen. This usually explains what the problem is. Here are some common problems and some advice about how to deal with them:

 The message may say that the Point Of Presence (see page 42) you are trying to connect to is busy. This means your access provider doesn't have a free modem to deal with your request to connect.

Try again a few times. If this doesn't work, try again later. Ask your access provider when the busiest times of day are, and avoid them.

If a message appears saying "timed out", it means your software has stopped trying to dial up a connection. Dial-up software is pre-set to make several attempts to connect, and in this case none of them were successful.

Try again a few times. Avoid trying to connect at peak times (see page 15).

The message may say that your "authentication" has failed. This means you have failed to gain permission to connect because the handshake was not recognized. There may be a problem with the remote computer, or you may have set up your Internet software incorrectly.

Call your access provider's helpline and ask for assistance.

 The message will say that you have entered the wrong password if you have typed in your password incorrectly or used the wrong password. Check your password and try again. Make sure that you use capital letters and small letters in the right places.

Opening your browser

If you haven't already started your browser, double-click on its icon to open it now.

When you start your browser, it automatically displays a particular Web page. This page is known as the default page and usually contains information about the manufacturer of the browser.

The default page will not appear in the browser window immediately, because it takes some time to send Web pages over the Net. For a few moments the central part of your browser window will remain blank.

Downloading

Gradually the default page appears in your browser window. It is being "downloaded" onto your computer, which means it is being stored in your computer's memory. The text on a Web page often downloads before the pictures.

When your browser is finding and receiving a page, the icon in the top right corner of the browser window moves. If you are using Netscape Navigator, you will see comets flying past a big N, and if you are using Microsoft Internet Explorer you will see a globe rotate.

The Netscape Navigator browser window

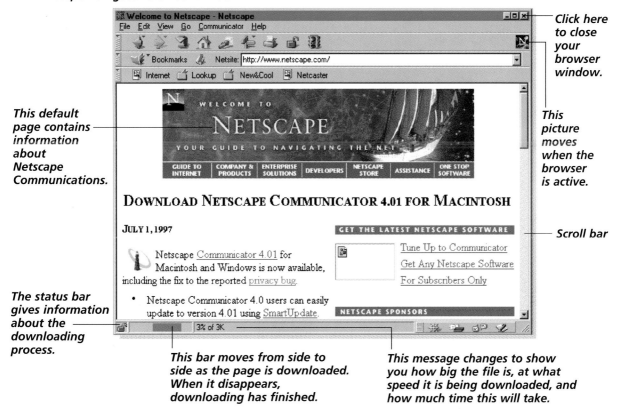

Click here to close your browser window.

This default page contains information about Netscape Communications.

This picture moves when the browser is active.

Scroll bar

The status bar gives information about the downloading process.

This bar moves from side to side as the page is downloaded. When it disappears, downloading has finished.

This message changes to show you how big the file is, at what speed it is being downloaded, and how much time this will take.

Disconnecting

Be careful. Your computer may not automatically disconnect from the Internet when you close your browser window.

To disconnect from the Net, go into your connection software window and click on the close or disconnect button or menu item.

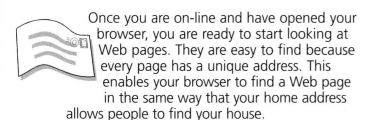

Once you are on-line and have opened your browser, you are ready to start looking at Web pages. They are easy to find because every page has a unique address. This enables your browser to find a Web page in the same way that your home address allows people to find your house.

Web addresses

A page's address is called a URL (Uniform Resource Locator). Here is an imaginary URL:

> http://www.usborne.co.uk

URLs may look confusing but they can be broken up to make them easier to understand.

> http:// www.usborne.co.uk

Web page URLs start with **http://** which stands for hypertext transfer protocol. This is the method that browsers use to read Web pages. This part of the URL is known as the protocol name.

> http:// **www.usborne.co.uk**

Web pages are stored on computers called servers or hosts. This part of the URL, known as the domain name, tells you about the host computer. This Web page is stored on a host called **usborne**.

The domain name may include codes that tell you about the organization that owns the host computer. In this example, **co.uk** specifies that the host is owned by a company from the United Kingdom.

Some Web page addresses have another part called the file path. This tells you exactly where the Web page is stored on the host computer. A Web page's URL has a file path when the page is stored inside a folder or directory.

Using URLs

It's easy to instruct your browser to find a Web page if you know the page's URL.

Try asking your browser to find the National Aeronautics and Space Administration (NASA) page. The URL for this page is: **http://www.nasa.gov/**.

The easiest way to tell your browser to find a new page is to click in the "Location" or "Address" box with your mouse, carefully type the URL and then press the Return key.

The Netscape Location box

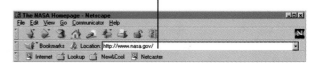

Your browser will contact the host computer and ask it to download a copy of the page onto your computer. Once a page has been downloaded, you can still look at it if you disconnect from the Internet.

⚠ Handle with care

If you type in an incorrect URL, your browser won't be able to find the page. When this happens, an error message similar to the one below appears on your screen.

Take care when you copy down a URL or type it into the location box. Don't leave any spaces between any of the letters. Make sure that you use capital letters and small letters in exactly the right places and don't mix up forward slashes **/** and dots **..**

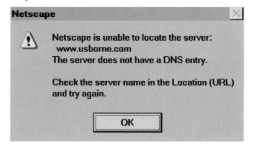

Web links

It is very easy to move around the Web because Web pages are interconnected. They contain words or pictures which link them to other Web pages containing related information. These words and pictures are known as "hyperlinks".

When you click with your mouse on a hyperlink, your browser automatically finds the particular page to which it links, and downloads this onto your computer. When you use a hyperlink to move to a Web page, you don't need to know the page's URL.

Words and pictures

Words which are hyperlinks can also be called hypertext. They are usually underlined or highlighted. Hyperlink pictures may be photographs or computer graphics. Some hyperlink computer graphics look like buttons. Others are small pictures which represent the page to which the hyperlink connects.

When your mouse is pointing to a hyperlink, your mouse pointer changes into a hand symbol like this. The URL of the page to which it links is displayed in your browser window.

This picture shows how you can use hyperlinks to jump between Web pages on the NASA Web site.

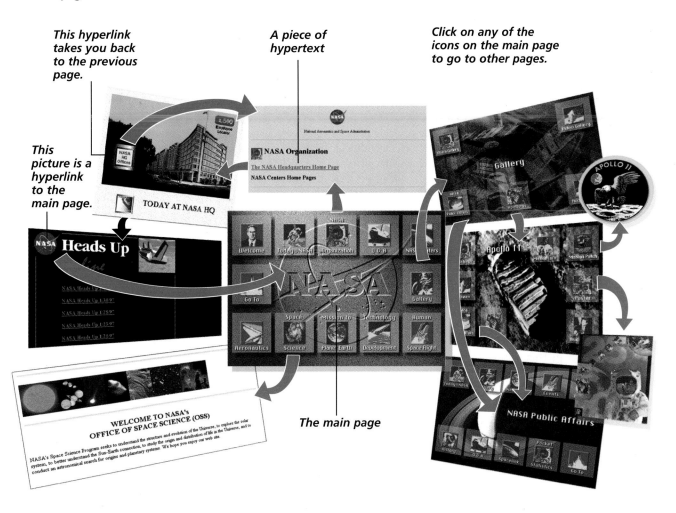

This hyperlink takes you back to the previous page.

A piece of hypertext

Click on any of the icons on the main page to go to other pages.

This picture is a hyperlink to the main page.

The main page

In this section you can find out some ways to save time and effort when exploring or "browsing" the Web.

Finding your way

It is easy to get lost when you are browsing the Web. You can get carried away following hyperlinks. Don't worry. Your browser automatically records which pages you have looked at during a browsing session.

Most browsers can show you a list of these pages. In both Netscape Navigator and Microsoft Internet Explorer, you can find this list under *Go* on the menu bar. To look again at a page that you have already downloaded, select its title in the list.

Most browsers also have buttons on the tool bar that you can use to retrace your steps. The examples shown below are from Netscape Navigator. Don't worry if you have a different browser; other browsers have tool bar buttons with very similar pictures or names.

 The *Back* button instructs your browser to show the page you looked at before the one it is currently displaying.

 Once you have moved back, you can use the *Forward* button. This tells your browser to show the page that you originally saw after the one you are currently looking at.

 The *Home* button on your browser's tool bar takes you back to your browser's default page. You can find out how to choose a different default page on page 30.

A second look

When you look at a page for a second time during a browsing session, the page appears in your browser window almost immediately. This is because your browser displays the copy of the page that it stored in your computer's memory. You don't have to wait for the page to be sent over the Internet again.

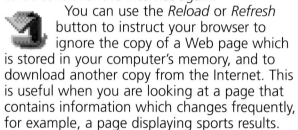 You can use the *Reload* or *Refresh* button to instruct your browser to ignore the copy of a Web page which is stored in your computer's memory, and to download another copy from the Internet. This is useful when you are looking at a page that contains information which changes frequently, for example, a page displaying sports results.

Web sites

A group of Web pages created by a person or an organization is called a Web site. The pages that make up a Web site are usually stored on the same host computer.

The main page of a Web site is called its home page. It usually tells you what you will find on the site, although it may not be the first page you see when you visit a site.

To help you to explore a Web site without getting lost, the pages that make up the site usually contain a hyperlink to the site's home page. This may appear as an icon, a button, or the word <u>home</u>.

This is the hyperlink that links pages on the LEGO Web site to its home page.

Don't confuse a home page hyperlink on a Web page with the *Home* button on your browser's tool bar.

Saving time

Some Web pages, especially those which contain pictures, take a long time to download. To save time, you can download the text on its own. Here's how you can instruct your browser to leave out the pictures.

 Select *Preferences...* from the *Edit* menu. A dialog box will appear on your screen. Choose *Advanced* from the directory tree on the left, then look at the check boxes on the right. If there is a mark next to the *Automatically load images* item, your browser will automatically download pictures. Make sure this item is not selected.

 Choose *Options* from the *View* menu. A dialog box will appear on your screen. On the *General* form, make sure that *Show pictures* is not selected.

When your browser downloads a text-only version of a Web page, it replaces the pictures with small icons.

This is the icon that Netscape Navigator uses to replace pictures.

If you decide that you want to see an image, click on the icon that replaces it, and your browser will download the picture.

Stop

You may start downloading a page which turns out to be uninteresting or offensive. You can stop downloading a page at any time by clicking the *Stop* button on your browser.

 Once you have pressed the *Stop* button, wait for your browser to respond. This may take a few seconds because your browser has to contact the host computer to cancel the downloading process. Don't keep clicking the *Stop* button or pressing the Return key. This will stop your browser from working temporarily and may even crash your computer.

Rush hour

If a lot of people are using the Net at the same time as you are, it may take a long time to download Web pages.

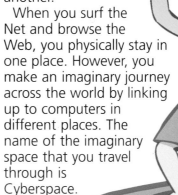

The Internet is like a road. When there is a lot of traffic on a road, the vehicles move more slowly than when there is only a little traffic. In the same way, the more people there are sending and receiving data over the Net, the slower the information travels.

If you want to get more done during the time you spend on-line, try using the Net late at night or early in the morning. You may find it is less busy.

Surfing in Cyberspace

In Internet slang "surfing the Net" means exploring the Internet, looking for interesting things to do. Some people say that this comes from the expression "channel surfing", which means rapidly changing television channels at random, looking for interesting programs.

A channel surfer switches between television channels just as a surfer catches one wave and then another. Similarly, a "Net surfer" moves around the Internet, jumping from one file to another.

When you surf the Net and browse the Web, you physically stay in one place. However, you make an imaginary journey across the world by linking up to computers in different places. The name of the imaginary space that you travel through is Cyberspace.

You may come across information on the Web that you want to look at again and again. You can either create short cuts to these Web pages or save the information onto disk.

Hotlists

A "hotlist" is a collection of short cuts to Web pages that you want to look at regularly. It's called a hotlist because "hot" is slang for something that is good or popular. The short cuts allow you to download particular Web pages without having to remember their URLs.

To add a page to a hotlist, display the page in your browser window, then follow the instructions below.

 In Netscape Navigator, the hotlist is called "Bookmarks". Select *Bookmarks* from the *Communicator* menu to make the *Bookmarks* menu appear. Then choose *Add Bookmark* from the *Bookmarks* menu.

 Microsoft Internet Explorer calls its hotlist "Favorites". Select *Add to Favorites...* from the *Favorites...* menu. A box may appear asking you to confirm your choice.

Using hotlists

To instruct your browser to download a page from your hotlist, follow the instructions below.

 You can find a list of your bookmarks in the *Bookmarks* menu. Click on the name of the Web page that you want to see, and your browser will download it.

 The *Favorites...* menu contains a list of short cuts to Web pages. Click on the name of the Web page that you want your browser to display.

To make it easier to find your short cuts, you can arrange them into folders. Click on *Edit Bookmarks...* or *Organize Favorites...* to display your hotlist window, then use the buttons or menus to create folders. To move a short cut into a folder, simply drag it to a new location.

Microsoft Internet Explorer's hotlist

Select a Web page from the list to download it.

Saving information

The Web is changing all the time. The URLs of some pages change and other pages are removed from the Web altogether. You may want to save some information into your computer's permanent memory or onto floppy disks so that you can look at it again later.

⚠ Copyright

Most of the information on the Web is available free. This doesn't mean that you can do what you like with it. If you want to publish either pictures or text in any way, (including elsewhere on the Web), you must first obtain permission from the person or company that owns the copyright. If you don't do this, you may be breaking the law. It is okay to save information onto your computer for personal use without asking.

Saving text

To save the text from a Web page that is displayed in your browser window, select *Save As...* from the *File* menu. Use the *Save As...* dialog box to give the page a filename and to instruct your computer where to save it.

The Save As... dialog box

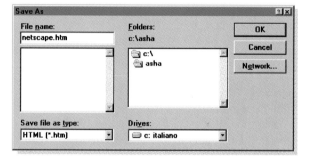

You must also choose how to save the page. Select one of the options listed under *Save as type*. When you save as *HTML*, the Web page keeps the same layout, but icons appear instead of pictures. If you select *Plain Text*, the copy you make will look very different from the Web page. For example, there will be no pictures and a different lettering and layout style will be used.

The Garfield page on the Web

The Garfield page saved as HTML

The same page saved as Plain Text

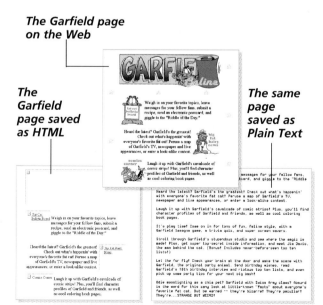

Pictures saved from:
http://www.pdimages.com/

Saving pictures

When you save a Web page, you have to save each picture on it separately. To save a picture, point at it with your mouse and press your mouse button down. (If you are using a PC, use the right button.) Select the item called *Save Image as...* (or something similar) from the menu which appears. Use the *Save As...* dialog box to choose a name and location for the picture.

Saving links

You can use a hyperlink to save a Web page without actually displaying the page in your browser window.

For example, you may want to save a selection of pages from a Web site that you have explored in a previous browsing session. Download the home page. You can now save other pages on that site using the hyperlinks which appear on the home page. Click on a hyperlink with your mouse and select *Save Link as* from the pop-up menu. Then use the *Save As...* dialog box as before.

Viewing saved information

You can look at any text and pictures you have saved when you are off-line. Launch your browser without connecting to the Net, then select *Open...* or *Open Page...* from the *File* menu. To display the *Open* dialog box, click on the *Browse...* or *Choose File...* button. Then use the dialog box in the usual way to find and select the file you want to see. If the file you are looking for isn't listed, change the entry under *Files of type* to *All Files*.

Searching the Web

You may need to use the Web to find out something specific, for example, for a school project. It can be hard to do this by clicking on hyperlinks at random. There are several programs on the Web, known as search services, that will help you find what you are looking for.

Search services

There are two types of search services: search engines (see pages 20 to 23) and directories. Directories are huge lists of hyperlinks to Web pages. The hyperlinks are organized into various categories according to the content of the pages they link to. For example, you will find hyperlinks to pages about music under the category "Entertainment".

Finding search services

Some browsers have a button which will lead you to a Web page containing a list of several different search services.

If your browser doesn't have this facility, you can find the URLs of search services in Internet magazines.

Here are the URLs of three useful directories:
Lycos at **http://a2z.lycos.com/**
Infoseek at **http://www.infoseek.com/**
Yahoo! at **http://www.yahoo.com/**.
It is a good idea to add them to your hotlist (see page 16).

Directory levels

Yahoo! is a popular directory.

Its home page has 14 large subject areas for you to choose from, including <u>Computers and Internet</u>, <u>Society and Culture</u> and <u>Health</u>. These are hyperlinks. When you click on one, you move down to another level of the directory, where there are smaller subject areas.

Clicking on one of these takes you to yet another level, with even smaller subject areas. This process of narrowing down the subject area is known as drilling down.

Using a directory

Say, for example, you want to use Yahoo! to find some pages containing information about natural history museums. On the home page, click on <u>Society and Culture</u>. A page will appear containing several categories which are all related to society and culture, including <u>Museums and Exhibits</u>.

Follow the <u>Museums and Exhibits</u> link. On the next level there are more options, for example <u>Art</u>, <u>Science</u>, and <u>Natural History</u>. When you click on the <u>Natural History</u> hyperlink, you will be presented with a list of hyperlinks to the home pages of natural history museums all over the world.

Using the Yahoo! directory to find natural history museums

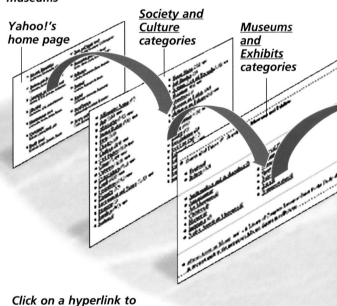

Yahoo!'s home page

Society and Culture categories

Museums and Exhibits categories

Click on a hyperlink to move down a level.

As you move through the directory levels, the subject areas become narrower.

Categories

Directories are compiled by people called editors who look at Web pages and decide which category each page should go in.

It may take you some time to get used to the way the pages in a directory are grouped together. Some topics fit naturally in more than one group. For example, pages about medicines could go under Health or Science.

When searching for information about a particular subject, it is a good idea to try all the possible categories in which it might be included.

Incomplete lists

Directories are not complete lists of all the pages on the Web. The Web is growing so rapidly that it is impossible for the editors of directories to classify all the new pages.

Editors have different methods of discovering Web pages to include in their lists. Many of them use computer programs to find pages which have recently been added to the Web.

Each directory is a unique selection of Web pages. If you can't find any information about a subject in one directory, you may find it in another one.

Web chaos

Search services are extremely useful because the Web is a very disorganized place. Nobody owns the Web and nobody controls it. Anyone can create a Web page or site without having to tell a central organization what information it contains or where it can be found.

Imagine a library where people were allowed to bring any book and place it wherever they wanted to, on the shelves or on the floor. It would be difficult to find a particular book. The Web is as chaotic as this imaginary library would be.

 Missing pages

Directories are so huge that it is difficult for editors to keep checking that the URLs listed are still correct. You may find a hyperlink in a directory which doesn't work, either because the page has been moved to another server, or because it has been removed from the Web altogether. When this happens, an error message will appear on your screen.

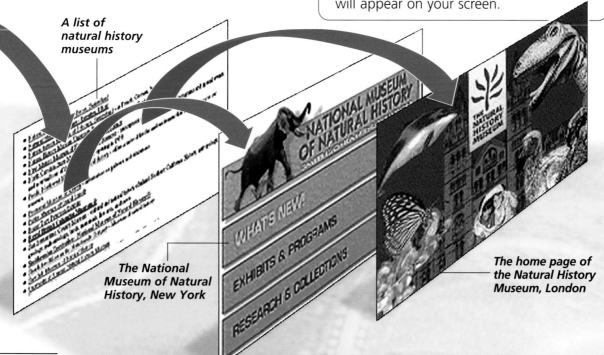

A list of natural history museums

The National Museum of Natural History, New York

The home page of the Natural History Museum, London

Word searches

Some search services allow you to search the Web for pages which contain particular words. They are known as search engines, or search indexes.

Key words

The "key words" of a Web page are the words which sum up its contents. For example, the key words of a Web page that explains what turtles eat are *turtles, food* and *eat*.

When you instruct a search engine to look for key words, it looks through an index of millions of Web pages that it has compiled. Any page the search engine finds which contains the word or words you require is known as a hit. The search engine will present the results of its search in a list. This may be one or several pages long, depending on how many hits there are.

Finding search engines

Here are the URLs of some useful search engines:
AltaVista at **http://www.altavista.digital.com/**
Open Text at **http://www.opentext.com/**
Webcrawler at **http://webcrawler.com/**
HotBot at **http://www.hotbot.com/**.

Simple searches

Say, for example, you wanted to use the AltaVista search engine to find out about turtles. Go to the AltaVista home page. You will see a blank strip known as a query box like the one shown here.

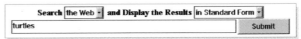

This is where you enter the key words. To do this, click in the space with your mouse, then type **turtles**. Next, click on the button which instructs the search engine to start the search. AltaVista calls this button *Submit*, but other search engines have a different names for it, such as *Search* or *Go Get It*.

After a few seconds, the search engine will produce a list of hits. Each item in the list includes a hyperlink to a Web page which contains the key word, and a short description of that page. This will help you decide which of the pages in the list is likely to be the most suitable. When you find an interesting-looking hyperlink, click on it to download the page.

A selection of the hits that AltaVista found for the word turtle

A results page

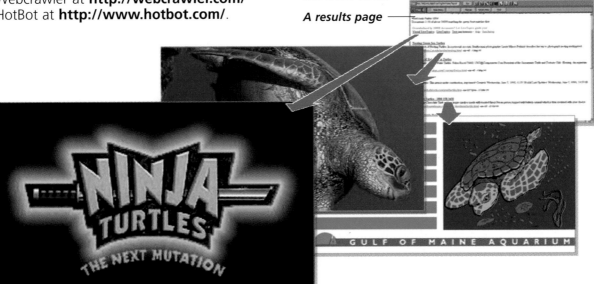

Expert searching

Sometimes results pages will contain thousands and thousands of entries. Many of these will have nothing to do with the subject you are interested in. For example, if you carry out a key word search on the word **rock**, the hits will include pages about music and about geology.

You can use a selection of words or symbols, known as operators, to give the search engine more precise instructions. This will reduce the chances of it turning up pages that don't interest you.

Check the instructions of a search engine to see whether you should use words or symbols. Some search engines have pull down menus from which you select the appropriate operator. With others, you have to type the operator into the query box.

Using operators

Here are some widely used operators:

 To make your instructions more specific, you can say you want two or more words to appear on the Web page. Type a plus sign before each word, or the word AND between the words. For example, if you want to find pages about rock music, you would type **+rock +music** or **rock AND music**.

You can also tell a search engine which words you don't want to appear on the page. Type a minus sign or the word NOT before any words you wish to avoid. For example, to find pages about any styles of music except jazz and classical, you would enter **music -jazz -classical** or **music NOT jazz NOT classical**.

If you enter more than one word in the query box without any operators, it usually makes the instruction less precise. Most search engines will look for pages which contain any of the words, and will find even more hits.

Spelling

Search engines look for the exact word or words you enter in the query box. It is very important, therefore, to make sure that you spell the word correctly. If you don't, you may find that there are no hits.

Search engines are usually "case-insensitive". This means that they don't distinguish between capital (upper case) letters or small (lower case) letters. So it doesn't matter which kind of letters you use when you type key words into a query box.

Creepy-crawlies

Search engines use special software to create their indexes. Each search engine has its own program that automatically builds up the index. The program constantly crawls across the Web, collecting information about Web pages. It also sorts the data into categories, and adds it to the index.

Some search engines are called crawlers, spiders or worms. These names refer to the different types of programs that the various search engines use to collect data about Web pages.

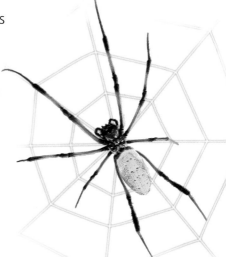

Expert searching

Here are some tips on how to make a search engine find exactly what you are looking for.

Phrases

You can instruct some search engines to search for pages where a group of words appear in a particular order.

AltaVista and WebCrawler will search for phrases if you enclose the words in quotation marks. For example, to find some Web pages about the Leaning Tower of Pisa, click with your mouse in a query box and type **"the Leaning Tower of Pisa"**.

You can also search for phrases using the Open Text search engine. You don't have to enclose the words in quotation marks. Instead, select *this exact phrase* from the drop-down menu to the left of the query box.

There are many pictures of the Leaning Tower of Pisa, Italy, on the Web.

Wild card

A search engine looks for the exact words you type into its query box. So when a search engine is looking for the word musician, it will not turn up pages that contain similar words such as music and musicians.

Some search engines, however, allow you to replace the different beginnings or endings of a word with a little star, called an asterisk. This symbol is often called the wild card. So, for example, if you type **music*** into a query box, this tells a search engine to look for any words which begin with music.

Searching by date

AltaVista can perform an "advanced" search. This means you can give it very specific instructions about the information you require. For example, you can use AltaVista to search for pages according to when they were put on the Web, or when the information on a page last changed. This is especially useful when you only want to find up-to-date information on a particular subject.

Say, for example, you wanted to use AltaVista to find information about fashion which was added to the Web over the last month. You would need to use AltaVista's advanced query form. To see this form, click on the *Advanced Search* button on the AltaVista home page.

AltaVista's advanced query form

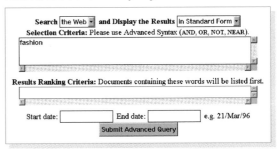

At the bottom of the form there are two boxes called *Start date:* and *End date:*. Enter whatever the date was one month ago in the first box, and today's date in the second box. Click on *Submit Advanced Query* to start the search.

Pictures from a fashion site found by AltaVista

Search results

You can often choose how you want the results of a search to be displayed. For example, you may be able to decide how many hits you want to see listed at a time, and how much information about them you want included on the results page.

Number of hits

Most search engines show 10 hyperlinks on each results page. So, a search which found 100 hits would produce 10 pages of results.

You can change the number of links you want to see. WebCrawler, for example, can display either 10, 25 or 100 results per page. On its home page, select the number you prefer from the drop-down menu which is located above the query box.

The WebCrawler query box

Select how many links you want to see on each results page here.

Each search engine works in a slightly different way, but most of them have similar drop-down menus on their home pages.

Descriptions

Search engines usually let you choose how much information you want to read about each hyperlink on their results pages. A description can range from a few words to a long paragraph.

WebCrawler, for example, allows you to choose between seeing only the titles of Web pages, or reading summaries of their contents. Select the option you prefer from a drop-down menu on its home page.

Order

Search engines present the results of a key word search in a particular order. The hits which best match your requirements appear on the first results page.

Search engines use different methods to decide which are the best matches. Some count how many times a key word appears on the page, others look at how near the key word is to the top of the page.

Changing the order

You may find that the hits that a search engine presents first are not the ones that interest you the most. When you perform an advanced search with AltaVista, you can decide which hits it should present first.

Say, for example, you want to find out about toys and games, but you are particularly interested in games. On the AltaVista advanced query form, enter **toys OR games** into the *Selection Criteria* box. Then type **games** into the *Results Ranking Criteria* box. AltaVista considers the word you type into this box to be the most important key word.

The search engine places the hyperlinks which lead to pages about games at the top of the results page. Links to pages about toys will appear farther down the results page.

One of the pages about toys found by AltaVista

Giving your opinion

This section shows two ways in which you can give your opinion about the sort of Web pages you want to see.

Personalized searches

You can personalize some search services so that they only list Web pages that they know you will find interesting. The Yahoo! search service can be personalized in this way.

To create your own version of Yahoo! go to: **http://edit.my.yahoo.com/config/login/**.

Creating your Yahoo!

Click on the *START YOUR OWN* button, then follow the on-screen instructions. You will have to complete two forms.

The first form asks you to invent a "login" name and a password. These allow Yahoo! to identify you when you use it. Both the login name and the password can be any combination of letters and numbers. It is a good idea to choose something you can remember easily, such as your name.

You will also have to provide personal information, such as your date of birth and your occupation. Enter the information required in the appropriate boxes, then click on *Register me now!* to continue.

The second form asks for information about your interests and preferences. Select the categories that interest you from the lists. Then click on *Use these interests*.

Select interesting categories on the second form.

Click on a box with your mouse.

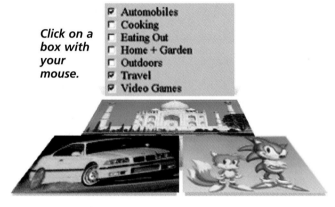

Your Yahoo!

The next page to appear explains what your personalized My Yahoo! contains and what the My Yahoo! icons represent. It's a good idea to save this page so you can refer to it whenever you need to (see page 16).

To see your personalized version of Yahoo! for the first time, click on the *Take me to My Yahoo!* button.

A personalized Yahoo page

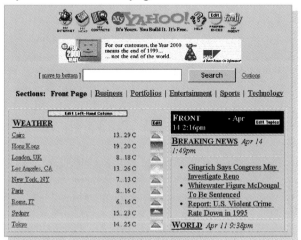

Your Yahoo! includes news pages, containing frequently updated news stories. The content of these pages depends on the categories that you selected on the second form. For example, if you selected Technology, you might find reports about new inventions on your personalized news pages.

 You will also find a unique search page called *My Internet*. This contains Web page recommendations and short cuts to your chosen Yahoo! directory categories.

Edit buttons

My Yahoo! contains several *Edit* buttons. You can use these to change the information you supplied when creating your Yahoo! To change any of the information that you entered on the first form, click on the *Edit* button which appears at the top of every page.

Logging in

The next time you want to see your Yahoo! pages, go to:
http://edit.my.yahoo.com/config/login/.
 Enter your login name and password in the space available, then click on the *Login* button. This instructs your browser to display your Yahoo!.

Intelligent Agents

Your Yahoo! includes an "intelligent agent" (IA). This is a special program which can learn about your likes and dislikes and find sites that are likely to interest you. Intelligent agents are often compared to dogs, because they track down Web sites on behalf of their master.

Training

Before you can use an IA, it has to be "trained" to judge pages on your behalf. To start training your Yahoo! agent, click on the *Firefly* icon. You will have to "rate" or tell your agent what you think of at least 20 Web sites.

Rating sites to train a Yahoo! agent

Select a description, such as great, ok or weak, from the drop-down menu.

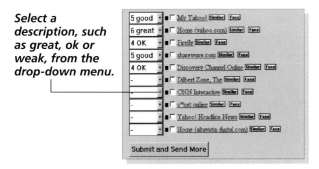

 When you have rated 20 sites, your agent will know more about what you like and dislike. It will then recommend Web sites to you. You can rate more than 20 sites if you want to. The more you train an IA, the more likely it is to recommend sites you will like.

Sending messages

Some Web sites contain a piece of hypertext which says comment, feedback, write to us or something similar. This means that the person who looks after the site, called the Webmaster, wants to receive comments and questions from the people who have visited the site.

 When you click on the hyperlink, your browser will download a Web page containing a form similar to the one shown below. You can use this form to send a message to the Webmaster.

 You may be asked to provide some personal information, such as your name and your computer address, known as your e-mail address (see below).

 Type your message into the main section of the form, then click on the *Send* or *Submit* button. Your message will be sent across the Internet to the Webmaster's computer.

A message form

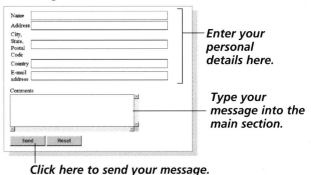

Enter your personal details here.

Type your message into the main section.

Click here to send your message.

E-mail

The process of sending messages from one computer to another is called electronic mail or e-mail. Everyone who is on the Net has a unique address to which you can send messages. Your access provider tells you what your e-mail address is when you open your account.

Downloading programs

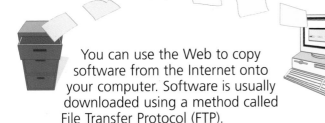

You can use the Web to copy software from the Internet onto your computer. Software is usually downloaded using a method called File Transfer Protocol (FTP).

FTP and the Web

FTP is the main way of sending files over the Net. Anything which can be stored on a computer – including pictures, sound clips, text files, and software – can be transferred by FTP. The files are stored on servers all over the world, called FTP sites. The URLs of FTP sites begin with **ftp://**.

Although FTP is a separate Internet facility from the Web, a Web page can contain a direct link to a file stored on an FTP site.

Finding programs on the Web

You can obtain a different browser, or a more recent version of a browser you already have, via the Web sites of browser manufacturers. These sites are often good places to look for other Web software too.
Microsoft's home page is at:
http://www.microsoft.com/.
Netscape Communications' home page is at:
http://www.netscape.com/.

Netscape Communications' banner

To download a program, look around the manufacturer's site for a hyperlink which starts the downloading process. For example, if you want a copy of Netscape Navigator, look for a button which is similar to the one below.

 ***Click on this button to download Netscape Navigator.***

To find other software, you can use a search engine (see pages 20 to 23). This is easier if you know the name of the program you are looking for. There is a search engine which searches only for software at:
http://www.shareware.com/.

Downloading preparations

Once you have clicked on a "download" hyperlink, a page will appear asking you to specify what type of computer you have, and what operating system (OS) it is running. (The OS is the group of programs which controls a computer, for example Windows or MacOS.)

You will also be asked which continent and country you live in. If the same program is stored on several different FTP sites, you will have to select a site to download from. Choose a site which is in your part of the world so that the file downloads as quickly as possible.

There are FTP sites in many different locations.

A page of FTP sites

You may find your browser can't connect to the FTP site you have chosen. This is because each FTP site has a maximum number of people who can use it at any one time. If this happens, try another site from the list.

Save As...

Before your computer starts downloading a program, a *Save As...* dialog box will appear on your screen. You must decide where to save the program on your computer's hard disk. If you have a "Programs" directory or folder, save the new software there. If not, you can create a new directory for any software you download. Click *OK* to confirm your choice.

Downloading

Once you have clicked *OK*, your browser contacts the FTP site, and begins downloading the program. A *Saving Location* window, like the one shown below, will appear on your screen. This gives you information about how the downloading process is progressing.

This is the URL of the FTP site where the program is stored.

```
Saving Location                     _ □ ×
Location:  ftp://sunsite.doc...ndows/n32e301.exe
Saving:    C:\TEMP\N32E301.EXE
Status:    1141K of 3547K (at 1.7K/sec)
Time Left: 00:23:59

■■■■■■■■■■■■                    32%

           [  Cancel  ]
```

This indicates how much of the program has already been downloaded.

Some programs are very large files, even when they have been compressed (see right). Try to download software when the Internet isn't busy so that it takes less time.

Compressed programs

Software files are usually compressed or "zipped". This means they have been reduced in size so they take up less space on an FTP site's hard disk. Compressed files can also be transferred from computer to computer more quickly than uncompressed files.

Before you copy any compressed program files from the Net onto your computer, you will need to have a program called a decompressor on your computer's hard disk. This program restores files to their original size so that your computer can use them.

A compressed program is like an inflatable boat with no air inside it. It's easier to store it and carry it around, but you can't use it. A decompressor is like the foot pump that you use to inflate the boat before using it.

How much does the software cost?

You'll have to pay for some of the software you find on the Net before you can download it. It usually costs as much as if you bought the same software in a store.

Some of the software which is available via the Web is free or costs very little.

Freeware This is software which is free for anyone to copy onto their computer and use.

Shareware This is software which you can download for free. By doing this, you automatically accept certain conditions. A common condition is that you will pay for a program if you decide to keep using it after an initial trial period of 30 days.

Trialware You can try out this software for free, but it contains a device which prevents you from using it fully. Some programs have features which don't work. Others contain a built-in timer which stops the whole program from working after an initial trial period. If you decide to keep the program, you pay the company who made it. They will send you a registration number. This is a code which makes the program work properly.

Betaware This is new software, that needs to be tested. It may not work properly. If you find a fault in a Beta program, you should tell the company that created it. Some beta programs are free; others are charged for.

Plug-ins

People who create Web pages sometimes make them more exciting by including sounds, moving images and animation. To do this, they use pieces of software called "plug-ins".

What is a plug-in?

A plug-in is a small program which works with a browser to give it an extra ability. For example, you can add a plug-in to your browser to enable it to show video clips.

If a Web page has been created using a particular plug-in, you will need to add that plug-in to your browser in order to see all the information on the page.

Animation

A plug-in called Shockwave™ enables you to see animations on Web pages. Shockwave also allows you to enjoy simple games and "interactive" features. Interactive means you can change things on the page by clicking with your mouse. For example, in the game shown below, you can "roll" the dice.

You can download Shockwave from: **http://www.macromedia.com/shockwave/**.

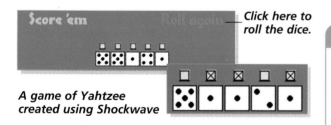

Click here to roll the dice.

A game of Yahtzee created using Shockwave

Video

Apple's Quicktime plug-in allows you to watch videos included on Web pages. You can also use it to see some animations and hear some sound effects. You will find Quicktime at: **http://www.quicktime.apple.com/**.

Videos are very big files. It may take a long time to download even a very short video clip.

Sound

The RealAudio® plug-in enables your browser to play sound effects and music clips on Web pages. You can also use it to hear Web radio and live concerts that are broadcast over the Web. The Real Audio home page is at: **http://www.realaudio.com/index.html**.

Using RealAudio to listen to Web radio

The RealAudio player lets you control what you hear.

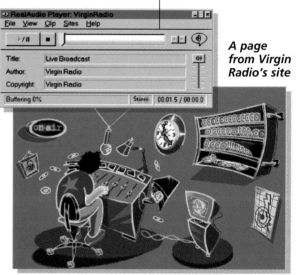

A page from Virgin Radio's site

Streaming

There are two ways in which sound and moving images can be sent from a Web server to your computer.

The first method of sending the information is called streaming. This is like watching TV or listening to the radio. You hear sounds or see images as your computer receives the data.

Alternatively, you may have to download all the data before you can hear or see the information. Once the data is stored on your computer, you can play the sounds or images over and over again, as if you had a CD or a video.

Downloading and installing

You may see a hyperlink on a site's home page which says something like "Get Shockwave". This means you need that particular plug-in to see all the information on the site. If you don't have the plug-in, you can usually download it by clicking on the hyperlink.

Alternatively, you can obtain a variety of plug-ins which work with your browser via your browser manufacturer's site.

When you download a plug-in, instruct your computer to save it in the "Temp" directory or folder on your computer's hard disk.

Once you have downloaded a plug-in, you will need to install it so that your browser knows it is on your computer. First shut down your browser, then open up the Temp directory, double-click on the plug-in's file name and follow the on-screen instructions.

When your browser was originally installed, it created a special directory or folder called "Plug-ins" on your computer's hard disk. You will find this plug-ins directory in the directory that has the same name as your browser.

During the installation of a new plug-in, your computer usually automatically stores it in the Plug-ins directory. Sometimes you have to tell your computer where this directory is.

Moving plug-ins

If you don't use a particular plug-in very often, you should move it from the Plug-ins directory to another part of your computer's hard disk. This is because plug-ins use up a lot of RAM (see page 6). If you keep a lot of plug-ins in the Plug-ins directory, your browser will work more slowly than usual. You can move a plug-in back to the Plug-ins directory whenever you want to use it.

Java

Some Web pages contain Java "applets". These are tiny programs written in a computer programming language called Java.

Java applets bring Web pages to life. They can contain moving charts and graphs which update themselves, short animations and interactivity.

An interactive java applet

TICKLE ME!

Use your mouse to "tickle" Elmo...

...then watch him wriggle!

To run a Java applet you need a browser, such as Microsoft Internet Explorer 3 or Netscape Navigator 2.1, which can understand Java. If your browser doesn't understand Java, you should download one which does from the Web (see pages 26 to 27).

Java is American slang for coffee. It's a suitable name for this programming language because coffee makes people feel energetic, and Java applets make Web pages more lively.

Some Web sites are available in two versions: one with Java applets and one without. The version which doesn't contain Java is sometimes called the "decaffeinated" version, because decaffeinated coffee doesn't make people feel more lively.

Personalizing your browser

You can change the way your browser looks and performs to suit your personal preferences. This is known as customizing your browser.

Your default page

If you find a Web page that you like and decide that you want to see it every time you launch your browser, you can make it your browser's default page (see page 11). Here's how to do this:

 Select *Preferences...* from the *Edit* menu. A dialog box will appear on your screen. Choose *Navigator* from the directory tree on the left so that the *Navigator* form appears on the right.

In the *Home page* section on the *Navigator* form, there is a box called *Location:*. Insert the URL of your chosen default page in this box, then click *OK*.

Personalizing Netscape Navigator's default page

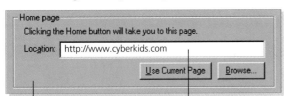

The Home page section   **Type the URL of your chosen page here.**

You will see your chosen page each time you launch your browser.

 You need to be on-line to change the default page. Download your chosen page so it appears in your browser window. Select *Options* from the *View* menu. A dialog box containing several forms appears on your screen. On the *Navigation* form, there is a section called *Customize*. Select *Start Page* from the drop-down menu, then click on the *Use Current* button. Finally, click *OK*.

Your tool bar

You can choose whether the buttons on your browser's tool bar have words or pictures on them. To do this, follow the instructions below:

 Use the *Appearance* form in the *Preferences...* dialog box. In the *Show toolbar as* section, you can select either Pictures Only, Text Only or Pictures and Text.

 The buttons on the tool bar always have both pictures and words on them. However, you can hide the words by dragging the bottom of the tool bar upwards, as shown below.

The Microsoft Internet Explorer tool bar

Drag the bottom of the tool bar up from here to hide the address box and the words on the tool bar.

Drag this label down to see the address box again.

The address box reappears.

Your browser's cache

Your browser stores a copy of every Web page it downloads in the "cache". This is an area of your computer's memory where frequently used data is stored.

Off-line viewing

You can look at a Web page which is stored in the cache without going on-line. This is called off-line viewing. It's a good idea to get used to viewing Web pages off-line if you have to pay for the time you spend on-line.

While you are on-line, let Web pages download fully, but read them quickly to decide which hyperlinks you want to follow. Once you have disconnected, you can study the pages in the cache for as long as you like.

The pages are stored in a directory or folder called Cache. On a PC, you will find this in the directory that has the same name as your browser. On a Macintosh, it is stored in the Preferences folder (inside the System folder).

To view a page off-line, double-click on its file name in the cache folder. Your browser will start automatically.

⚠ Numbers

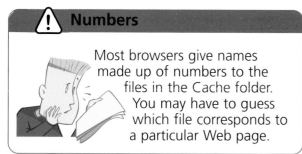

Most browsers give names made up of numbers to the files in the Cache folder. You may have to guess which file corresponds to a particular Web page.

Cache size

Only part of the cache is set aside for your browser. Once its part is full, your browser will delete some of the pages which are stored there in order to make room for new pages. You may want to make your browser's part of the cache bigger so that your browser can store more pages. This will reduce the amount of time you spend on-line, because it takes less time for your browser to fetch a page from the cache than from a Web server.

Changing the cache size

You can only make your browser's cache bigger if your computer has some free RAM (see page 6). To set aside more RAM for your browser's cache, follow the instructions below. Be careful not to increase the size of the cache too much, as this may slow down your computer.

 Open the *Preferences...* dialog box and find the *Cache* form. (It's under *Advanced* in the directory tree.) The box called *Disk Cache* shows how many bytes have been set aside by your browser for storing downloaded pages. To make the cache bigger, highlight the number in the box and type in a larger number. It is a good idea to increase the number 500 KB at a time.

 Open the *Options* dialog box and click on the tab of the *Advanced* form. Then click on the *Settings* button in the *Temporary Internet files* section. In the window that appears, you can see what percentage of the hard disk space is being used. To make the cache bigger, move the marker as shown below. It is best to adjust the size of the cache 2% at a time.

Use this dialog box to adjust the size of Microsoft Internet Explorer's cache.

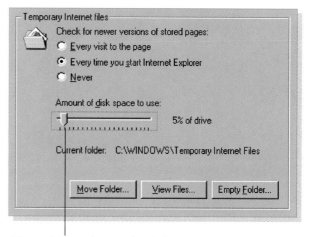

Move this marker to the right to make the cache bigger.

Buying and selling on-line

You can buy a wide variety of things on the Web, such as toys, tickets, clothes, cameras, pizza, and paintings. These pages shows how companies use the Web to find customers.

Shopping malls

People often buy a lot of different things, such as shoes, gifts, food and books, in one shopping expedition. To do this, it is easier to go to a place called a shopping mall, where you can buy all these things under one roof.

There are shopping malls on the Web too. Each "on-line mall" is a Web site which contains hyperlinks to a wide variety of Web pages where you can buy things. A good example is at:
http://www.imall.com/.

Each on-line mall has a "site directory". This is a list of hyperlinks to all the shopping pages in the mall. The hyperlinks are usually categorized according to what the pages sell. Hyperlinks to Web pages that sell footballs, for example, are listed under "sports".

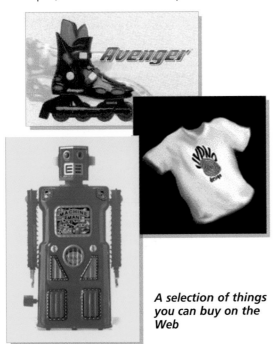

A selection of things you can buy on the Web

Going shopping

Each shopping site contains information about all the things you can buy. You will often see photographs of the products. Some sites even use 3-D pictures so you can look at an object from different angles.

When you find something that you want to buy, you have to order it and pay for it.

This 3-D dinner service comes from the Virtual Reality Mall (http://www.vr-mall.com/).

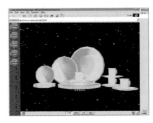 

You can look at it from any angle you choose.

Ordering

At some shopping sites, you select any items you want as you browse. You usually do this by placing a mark in a box next to a description of an item. This process is known as carting. At other sites, you make your selection after you have finished looking around the site. To do this, you complete an order form.

A page from a shopping site

A CD ——

This tells you how much the CD costs.

Click here to download an order form and to pay.

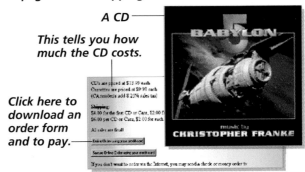

To finish making your order, follow the on-screen instructions. You will have to provide some information, such as your name and address, so that the goods you buy can be delivered to your house.

Paying

To pay for goods ordered over the Web, you need a bank account. Here are the two most common ways of paying over the Net:

 Credit cards This is the most widely used payment method. You enter credit card details onto a payment form on the Web site. This information is then used to remove the money from your bank account.

 Before you give out your credit card details, make sure you can see a picture of an unbroken key somewhere on the Web site. This tells you that the information you supply will be "encrypted" before it is sent across the Net. This means it will be turned into a complicated secret code which only the person to whom you send the information knows how to decode.

 Digital money Digital money is made of computer data but it has the same value as ordinary paper and metal money.

Before you go shopping on the Web, you withdraw digital money from your bank account via the Internet and store it on your computer's hard disk. (Ask your bank which software you need to do this.) When you want to buy something through a shopping site, you send the digital money over the Internet to the computer of the person that you have to pay.

⚠ Computer crime

 Some people don't think it is safe to send private information over the Internet, even if it is encrypted. Criminals may be able to intercept an e-mail or a Web page which contains your credit card details. If they worked out how to decode the information, they could use it to steal money from your bank account.

Entrance fees

Some of the information on the Web is not free for you to use. You have to pay before you can look at it.

For example, to play the games on the Entertainment Online site, you have to "subscribe". This means you pay a monthly fee which allows you to play them as often as you like. However, you can look at other information on the site free of charge.

Entertainment Online is at: **http://www.e-on.com/**.

Two of the games you can play at the E-On® site

Scottish Open Golf

Speedball II

Other sites use a system called micropayment. You pay a small amount for each piece of information that you use. Some games sites ask you to pay each time you play a game.

Advertisements

Many Web pages carry advertisements. Advertising is the main reason that most of the information and search services on the Web are free to use.

Companies pay to advertise their products and services on other people's Web pages. This money is usually used to maintain and improve the Web pages where the advertisements are displayed.

Your own Web page

Anyone can add information to the Web, including you. Why not tell the world about yourself? Create your own page and put it on the Web for everyone to see.

Getting started

Using an ordinary word processing program, type a document which contains everything you want to say on your page. People usually include information about where they live, their families and friends, and their interests.

A selection of personal Web pages

⚠ Shhhh

Don't include any personal details, such as your address or phone number, on your Web page. Remember that anyone in the world can see the information. It's a good idea to reread what you have written and think whether you would tell this information to a complete stranger. If you wouldn't, don't put it on your Web page.

Web page code

To make a Web page, you need to use a code called Hypertext MarkUp Language (HTML). This is a set of instructions which you add to a word-processed document to turn it into a Web page.

HTML instructions tell a browser how to display the information a Web page contains. When people look at your page on the Web, they won't see the instructions.

The HTML for a particular Web page is called its source. To see the source of a Web page which is displayed in your browser window, select *Page Source* or *Source* from the *View* menu. Don't be scared by what you see; HTML code looks confusing, but it's easy to use.

A Web page

The source for the Web page

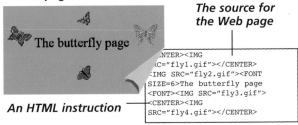

An HTML instruction

Tags

An HTML instruction is called a tag. Tags usually come in pairs – an opening tag and a closing tag. The opening tag comes before the words which are affected by the instruction and the closing tag comes after them. In this example, the tags affect the word Bruno.

An opening tag **<B>Bruno</B>** *A closing tag*

Tags are always put inside these two symbols < >. Notice that closing tags always contain a forward slash / .

First tags

All Web page sources start with the same set of tags. Type this sequence at the top of your document, replacing "Bruno's page" with whatever you want your page to be called.
```
<HTML>
<HEAD>
<TITLE>Bruno's page</TITLE>
</HEAD>
```
The title doesn't appear on the Web page. It appears in the title bar of your browser, as shown below.

🌐 Bruno's page - Microsoft Internet Explorer
File Edit View Go Favorites Help

Contents

The words and pictures which appear inside your browser window are called "the body" of the page. Type <BODY> above all the text that you typed before you added any HTML tags. Then type </BODY> at the end of this text.

This information will appear on the Web page.

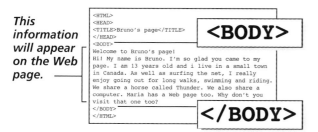

```
<HTML>
<HEAD>
<TITLE>Bruno's page</TITLE>
</HEAD>
<BODY>
Welcome to Bruno's page!
Hi! My name is Bruno. I'm so glad you came to my
page. I am 13 years old and i live in a small town
in Canada. As well as surfing the net, I really
enjoy going out for long walks, swimming and riding.
We share a horse called Thunder. We also share a
computer. Maria has a Web page too. Why don't you
visit that one too?
</BODY>
</HTML>
```

<BODY>

</BODY>

Special effects

Some word processors have tool bar buttons and menu items which allow you to make some words bigger than others, and to put words in **bold** or *italics*.

When you are creating a Web page source, you can't use these tools. The effect won't be seen by a browser. Instead, you add tags which tell the browser to create special effects. Here are some tags you might find useful:

B   <B>Bruno</B> makes the letters inside the tags bold, like this: **Bruno**

<I>Bruno</I> makes the letters inside the tags italic, like this: *Bruno*   *I*

A^A   <FONT SIZE=7>Bruno</FONT> makes the letters very big and <FONT SIZE=1>Bruno</FONT> makes them very small. You can also use SIZE=2, SIZE=3 and so on for different sized letters.

These letters are size 7.   *These letters are size 4.*

Bruno 7 Bruno 4

The actual size may vary according to your computer.

Single tags

Some tags, called standalones, have only one part. For example, when you type <BR> this tells the browser to start a new line, and when you type <P> this tells the browser to start a new paragraph. To tell the browser to draw a horizontal line, type <HR>.

Standalones divide up the information on the page.

Welcome to Bruno's page!
Hi! My name is Bruno. I'm so glad you came to my page.

I am 13 years old and I live in a small town in Canada. As well as surfing the Net, I really enjoy swimming and riding.

I have a sister called Maria who also enjoys riding. We share a horse called Thunder. We also share a computer.

Maria also has a Web page. Why don't you visit that one too?

<P>   **
**   **<HR>**

Saving your page

At the very end of your source document, type </HTML>. This tells a browser that this is the end of the Web page.

When you save your work, it is important to enter the correct information into the *Save As...* dialog box. First make sure *Plain Text* or *Text documents* is selected in the *Save file as type* field. Then give your file a name which is no more than 8 letters and numbers long. When you type in a file name, use only lower case letters and add the file extension .htm. This tells a browser that the file is a Web page.

Checking your page

It's a good idea to look at your page through your browser to make sure you have written the HTML correctly. First launch your browser without connecting to the Net, then open your Web page using the appropriate command in your browser's *File* menu.

You may want to make some changes to the information on your page or to the HTML code. To do this, open your page in your word processing program, alter it, save the changes and close the file. To see what the changes look like, open the file in your browser again.

Advanced page design

You can make your page more attractive and interesting by adding bright backgrounds and pictures. You can also add hypertext links to other Web pages.

Bruno

Backgrounds

You can give your page a different, more exciting background. To do this, you need to insert some extra code into the opening part of the body tag (see page 35). If you want the background of your page to be yellow, for example, you would replace <BODY> with this:
<BODY BGCOLOR ="EEE9BF">

In this tag, EEE9BF is a code which tells the browser to use a pale yellow background. To tell your browser to use a different background, use another code. There is a different code for most shades.

Here are the codes for some other backgrounds.

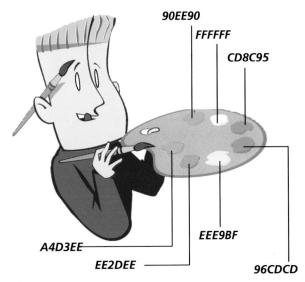

90EE90
FFFFFF
CD8C95
A4D3EE
EE2DEE
EEE9BF
96CDCD

You can find out more codes on the following Web page:
http://www.imagitek.com/bcs.html.

Pictures

Before you can add a picture to your Web page, it must exist in digital format. This means it must exist in a form that can be stored on a computer.

To convert a picture which is on a piece of paper to digital format, you need to use a machine called a scanner. Companies which provide a photocopying service or develop photographs often own scanners. They may scan your pictures for you, or show you how to use their machine. When a picture has been scanned, it should be saved with a .gif or a .jpg extension.

A scanner

Inserting a picture

Imagine you want to include a picture saved as "bruno.gif" in your Web page. Store the picture file in the same directory as the .htm file. Open the source file and insert this tag:
<IMG SRC="bruno.gif"> where you want the picture to appear.

Welcome to Bruno's page!

Hi! My name is Bruno. I'm so glad you came to my page.

I am 13 years old and I live in a small town in Canada. As well as surfing the Net, I really enjoy swimming and riding.
I have a sister called Maria who also enjoys riding. We share a horse called Thunder. We also share a computer.

A Web page with a picture and its source

Source

A picture tag

```
<IMG SRC="bruno.gif">
```

```
./TITLE>
Welcome to Bruno's page!</FONT>
am Bruno. I'm so glad you came to my

<BR>I am 13 years old and i live in a small town in
Canada. As well as surfing the net, I really enjoy
going out for long walks, swimming and riding.
<P>I have a sister called Maria who also enjoys
riding. We share a horse called Thunder. We also
share a computer.
<IMG SRC="bruno.gif">
</BODY>
</HTML>
```

Hyperlinks

You may want to add hypertext links from your Web page to other pages which you particularly like. Before you add the tag which does this, you need to decide which words you want to turn into hypertext.

Suppose you wanted to turn the word "Maria" in the sentence "Maria also has a Web page" into hypertext. The opening part of the link tag contains the URL of the page to which you wish to link. Imagine that the URL for Maria's page is:
http://www.usborne.com/maria/.

To create a link to this page, you would type:
<A HREF="http://www.usborne.com/maria/"> Maria</A> also has a Web page.

If you look at your Web page through your browser, you will see that the word "Maria" has been turned into hypertext, as shown below.

A piece of hypertext

Maria also has a Web page. Why don't you visit that one too?

If you have more than one Web page, you can use hypertext tags to link them up.

Find out more

There are many other ways you can make your Web page more exciting, such as including video. You will find magazines, books and Web pages that deal with other aspects of Web page design. You can also learn how pages on the Web have been created by looking at their sources (see page 34).

Web editors

Software packages which make it easier to create Web pages are known as Web editors. You don't need to know HTML code to create a page using a Web editor.

You can use a search engine such as **http://www.download.com/** to find a Web editor which you can download from the Net.

Alternatively, you can download Luckman's WebEdit. You can find this program at:
http://www.luckman.com/.

A Web editor called Web Edit

On the Web

Once you have created your Web page, you need to store it on a Web server so that other Web users can see it. Most Internet access providers provide their customers with some space on one of their server's hard disks at little or no cost.

You can use FTP (see page 26) to put your Web page on a Web server. This process is known as uploading. Telephone your access provider and ask them to explain how to upload your page onto their Web server. Your access provider will also provide you with a URL for your Web page.

Publicity

Make sure other Web users can find your page by telling a few search services about it.

To register your Web page with a search engine, go to its home page and look for a hyperlink called Add to or Add URL. Click on this hyperlink and fill in the form which appears in your browser window.

To save time, you may want to visit a site which sends your page's URL to several different search engines for you. To do this go to Submit It at:
http://www.submit-it.com/.

Virtual Reality on the Web

Virtual Reality (VR) is the use of computers to create objects and places which appear to be real. You can find some examples of Virtual Reality on Web pages.

Virtual worlds

Anything which is created by Virtual Reality is known as a virtual world. A virtual world may be a planet, a group of buildings, or even a single room. It can be a copy of something which exists in the real world, or it can be something which is entirely imaginary. A virtual world is created with 3-D images.

On page 43, you will find the URLs of Web pages which contain hyperlinks to virtual worlds. It usually takes a few minutes to download one.

A virtual world appears on your computer screen as a 3-D picture.

This virtual world is a copy of Piccadilly Circus, London.

This one is an imaginary space station.

Inside a virtual world

Use your mouse, or the arrow keys on your keyboard, to travel through a virtual world. You can explore the space in front and behind, on either side, or above and below you.

Wherever you go in a virtual world, it feels as though you are moving. This is because your surroundings change, just as they would in the real world. For example, when you approach an object, it appears to become bigger.

To make you feel as though you are moving closer, your computer draws a sequence of images. In each new image, the objects in front of you are slightly larger than in the previous one.

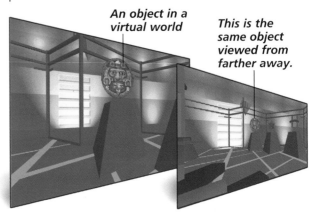

An object in a virtual world

This is the same object viewed from farther away.

Your computer has to draw each new image very quickly so you feel as if you are moving. If you have to wait for a new image to appear, the effect is lost. As a result, the images are usually quite simple.

As you explore a virtual world, you don't see yourself on your computer screen, you see only your surroundings.

Hardware and software

To experience virtual worlds, you need a powerful computer (at least a 486DX66 with 16MB of RAM), a fast modem (at least 28.8 bps) and a video card.

You also need a browser that can handle a programming language called Virtual Reality Modeling Language (VRML). One such browser is Netscape Navigator 3.0. VRML is the language that is used to create most virtual worlds on the Web. If you don't have a VRML browser, you will need to obtain a VRML plug-in for your browser (see page 28).

To visit a virtual world called AlphaWorld, you need a computer with a Pentium processor.

Meeting places

One of the most exciting things about virtual worlds on the Web is that you can use them to meet other people. A virtual world where you can see and communicate with other Web users is known as a 3-D chat room.

To enjoy 3-D chat rooms, you will have to download some software. You can find out more about this at:
http://www.activeworlds.com/ or **http://www.onlive.com/utopia/**.

This 3-D chat room is based on Yellowstone National Park in the USA.

Avatars

Before you enter a 3-D chat room, you have to choose an "avatar". This is a character which will represent you in the virtual world. It may look like a person or an animal or an imaginary creature, such as an alien.

Avatars from a virtual world called Utopia

You use your arrow keys or your mouse to instruct your avatar to move. As you explore a 3-D chat room, you will see avatars which represent the other people who are visiting that particular virtual world at the same time as you.

Communication

In some chat rooms, you use your keyboard to type what you want to say to the people you meet. Your words appear on the screen for them to read. In others, you can actually hear what other people are saying and talk to them.

Avatars chatting in AlphaWorld

Bill	Where are you from?
Jaques	Paris
Bill	I'm from Toronto.

Read what they are saying here.

CD-ROMs

You can also buy virtual worlds on CD-ROM, which you can explore on- or off-line. The CD-ROM contains links to a Web server. If you go on-line to explore a world, you may meet other people there. You can only meet other people when you are on-line because the data which tells your computer what they are doing and saying is sent over the Net.

⚠ VRML problems

There are many different VRML browsers and plug-ins. Some virtual worlds only work with particular browsers and plug-ins. The only way to find out if your software can handle a virtual world is to visit it and see what happens.

If you can't see anything or if you can't move around, this means you don't have the right software for that particular world. You will have to download a different browser or plug-in and try again. Alternatively, look for a world which works with the software you already have.

Future developments

Companies that develop software keep inventing and introducing exciting new ways of presenting information on the Web.

Many of the things that you will be able to do with the Web in the future are already possible with very advanced computers. The technology will become available to most users once computers in homes, schools and offices become more powerful, and data can be transferred more quickly.

Net links

The computers that make up the Net are linked in various ways: by telephone wires, by cables, and by satellites. Each type of link can transfer a maximum amount of data per second. This maximum limit is called bandwidth. It is measured in bps (see page 7).

Cable and satellite links are "high-speed" Internet connections. This means they have a large bandwidth. Most Net users still have data delivered to their computers by ordinary telephone wires. Some people, however, use high-speed connections.

High-speed connections

The cables which are used to transfer data across the Internet are made of thin glass strands. They use pulses of light to transmit information. To use cables to send and receive Net data, you need a cable modem.

Pulses of light passing along thin glass strands

A cable modem

Information can be sent along these cables thousands of times faster than along ordinary copper telephone wires.

Satellite links have an even larger bandwidth than cables. Internet data is transferred by communications satellites. These are spacecraft which circle Earth, automatically sending and receiving information.

A communications satellite

Improving links

To increase the speed of data transfer over the Net, telephone lines are gradually being replaced by cable and satellite links. This is a very long and expensive process, but it will make the Internet more efficient.

Web TV

You will soon be able to watch TV on Web pages. One of the great things about Web TV is that it will be interactive, which ordinary TV isn't. When you watch a news bulletin on ordinary TV, the information that you hear and see has been chosen by a reporter. You can't ask for more information about the things that interest you, or ask questions about the things you don't understand.

With Web pages, you can make choices about what information you require by clicking on hyperlinks. Similarly, with Web TV, you will be able to choose what you watch by clicking on hyperlinks.

For example, if you are watching a program about a planet called Saturn, and you don't know where it is, you will be able to click on a hyperlink to find out.

You will be able to find out more about Saturn using hyperlinks on Web TV.

Virtual worlds

Some Net surfers are disappointed when they visit virtual worlds on the Web (see pages 38 and 39). They expect to find places in which there is a great deal to be discovered. In most virtual worlds, however, there are not many places to explore, and the pictures that make up the surroundings are not very detailed. However, as the speed at which data is transferred over the Internet increases, the quality of virtual worlds on the Web will improve.

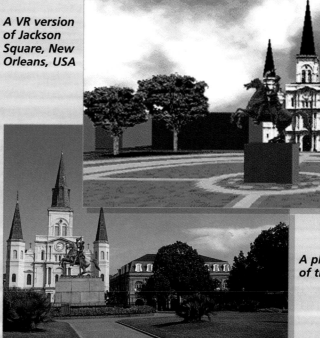

A VR version of Jackson Square, New Orleans, USA

A photograph of the square

Compare the Virtual Reality Jackson Square to the real one. The 3-D image is not as detailed as the photograph.

Storage devices

On page 39 you found out that a virtual world can be stored on CD-ROM. Soon, virtual worlds will also be available on Digital Video Discs (DVD-ROM).

A DVD-ROM is a device on which a huge amount of information can be stored. A DVD-ROM looks like a CD-ROM, but it can hold up to 26 times more data.

Virtual worlds stored on DVD-ROM will be more detailed than the worlds that are currently available. Some DVD-ROM virtual worlds will contain links to Web servers. If you explore one of these worlds when you are on-line, you will be able to meet other Web users in highly realistic Virtual Reality environments. You will also be able to vary your environment by temporarily adding new objects. For example, if your virtual world was a forest, you could introduce birds that fly overhead.

Digital video discs

This is a DVD-ROM drive, which is a device which reads DVD-ROMs. It fits into a computer's processing unit.

Providing access

Access providers are companies that you can pay in order to gain access to the Internet. There are two main types: on-line services and Internet Access Providers (IAPs).

An on-line service provides you with access to its own private network as well as the Internet. This private network will offer various services including discussion groups, shopping facilities, and information.

IAPs will only provide you with a gateway to the Internet but they are often cheaper than on-line services.

Choosing an access provider

There are many different access providers and more are appearing all the time. Each company offers a different service, so you should spend some time telephoning different companies to find the one which is best suited to your needs. You can find out the telephone numbers and addresses of access providers in Internet magazines and in telephone books.

Here are some questions that you may want to ask before deciding which company to use:

How much will I have to pay?
Different companies charge for their services in different ways. Some ask for a set monthly fee regardless of how much time you spend on-line. Others charge according to the amount of time you spend on-line. Some companies combine these two methods. They charge a monthly fee for a fixed amount of time on-line, and then charge for any extra time by the hour.

Try to avoid companies which make you pay a start-up cost. This is a fee you pay to open the account. You will lose this money if you decide to change access providers.

Can I dial up a connection locally?
Some access providers have computers that give access to the Net all over the country Other companies only have them in one area.

Make sure that you can dial up a connection to the access provider's computer by making a local telephone call. If you have to make a long distance call every time you dial up a connection, it will be more expensive.

A computer which acts as a point of access to the Net can be called a node or a Point of Presence (POP).

When can I call your helpline?
Most access providers have a telephone helpline. You can call the helpline for advice on any problems you may have connecting. Make sure the helpline is open at the times when you are likely to be using the Net.

Do you have enough modems?
An access provider's computer needs a free modem in order to connect each person who dials up. You will not be able to connect to the Internet if all the access provider's modems are busy dealing with other people's requests to connect.

Ask how many modems the access provider has per customer. It is best to choose a provider which has at least one modem for every 20 customers.

Do you offer free Web space?
If you want to put your own page on the Web, you will need to store it on the hard disk of a Web server. Some access providers include some free space on a server as part of their basic charges. Others will ask you to pay extra for Web space.

Useful addresses

Here is a selection of Web sites which you might like to visit. Some of them contain more information about things which are mentioned in this book. Others are sites which are featured in the book or which are particularly interesting to visit.

Further information

About intelligent agents:
http://www.agentware.com/
http://firefly.com/

About digital money:
http://www.digicash.com
http://www.cybercash.com

About safety issues:
http://www.safekids.com/

About Real Audio sites and live concerts on the Web:
http://www.timecast.com/

Addresses of access providers all over the world:
http://www.thedirectory.org/

Addresses of virtual worlds:
http://planet9.com/
http://hiwaay.net/~crispen/vrml/worlds.html

Software

A search engine for all types of programs:
http://www.download.com/

A search engine for shareware:
http://www.shareware.com/

Programs for compressing and inflating files:
PKZip
http://pkware.com/
Winzip for Windows
http://www.winzip.com/
Stuffit for Macs
http://www.spiritone.com/info/mac.html

Entertainment

Disney's home page:
http://www.disney.com/

Nintendo's home page:
http://www.nintendo.com/

A Web Radio station:
http://www.virginradio.co.uk/

Doom and Quake computer games:
http://www.idsoftware.com

⚠ Safety issues

Anyone can use the Internet and the Web. Unfortunately not everyone uses them responsibly. Here are some ways of making browsing the Web a safe activity.

 Viruses are programs which are deliberately made to destroy or change data. They can be transferred from computer to computer via networks or disks.

Make sure you have a virus checking program on your computer before you start downloading software from the Web. Use it to check each progam that you download.

 People can add whatever information they like to the Web. You may come across some information that upsets or offends you. Remember that you can use the Stop button to stop downloading any information that you don't want to look at.

Alternatively, you can use a program known as a filter which will censor Web pages for you. This means it will prevent your browser from downloading pages which contain offensive words. A good example is Cyber Patrol:
http://www.cyberpatrol.com/

Web words

Here are the meanings of some of the Web and Internet words that you may come across.

Some of the words in this list have two meanings: a general meaning and a specific Web or Net meaning. You will only find the specific Web or Net meanings here.

Any word that appears in *italic* type is defined elsewhere in the glossary.

applet A tiny program written in *Java*.

application A program that allows you to do something useful with your computer.

avatar A small on-screen, movable picture which represents the body of a computer user in a *virtual world*.

bandwidth The capacity of a link between computers to transfer data, measured in *bits per second (bps)*.

betaware Newly written programs that are made available to be tested by users.

bit The smallest amount of computer information.

body The part of a *Web page* which appears inside the main part of a *browser* window.

bps (bits per second). The unit used to measure how fast data is transferred across a link between two computers.

browser A piece of *software* which finds and displays *Web pages* and other documents stored on the *Internet*.

bug An imperfection in a computer program.

cache The part of a computer's memory where *Web pages* that have been *downloaded* are stored temporarily.

clickstream The path you take around the *Web* by clicking on *hyperlinks*.

Cyberspace The imaginary space that you travel around in when you use the *Net*.

decaffeinated or decaf Not containing *Java applets*.

decompressor A program used to expand compressed files.

dial up The use of telephone lines to connect a computer to another computer which is on the *Internet*.

digital money Money made up of computer data.

directory A list of *hyperlinks* to *Web pages* which are organized into categories.

DNS (Domain Name System). A system of giving computers on the *Net* names that are unique, and easy for users to remember.

domain Part of the name for an *Internet* computer that specifies its location and what sort of organization owns it.

down A word used to describe a computer which isn't functioning.

download To copy files, such as *Web pages* or programs, from a computer on the *Net* to your computer.

drilling down Going through the levels of a *directory*, choosing narrower and narrower subject areas.

e-mail (electronic mail). A way of sending messages from one computer to another.

encryption Using a complex code to keep information secret.

FAQ (Frequently Asked Questions). A *Web page* which contains the answers to the questions most commonly asked by visitors to a *Web site*.

freeware *Software* that is free to use

FTP (File Transfer Protocol). The system used to transfer files from one computer to another over the *Net*.

graphics Pictures created using a computer.

handshake A signal sent by a *modem* to an *access provider*'s computer in order to obtain permission to connect to the *Net*.

hardware The equipment that makes up a computer or a *network*.

header A piece of information at the beginning of a computer document.

A *Web page* header, for example, contains information about the *title* of the Web page.

helper application A program which is automatically launched when a *browser* needs help performing a particular task. Helper applications are used for files which are too big or complicated for *plug-ins* to handle.

hit A page found by a *search engine* which contains the *key words* entered into its *query box*. It can also mean when someone looks at a *Web site*. The number of hits a site receives can be counted to see how popular the site is.

home page An introductory page which contains links to other pages on a *Web site*.

host A computer connected to the *Net* which holds information that can be accessed by Net users.

HTML (HyperText Mark-Up Language). The computer code added to word-processed documents to turn them into *Web pages*.

HTTP (HyperText Transfer Protocol). The language computers use to transfer *Web pages* over the *Net*.

hyperlink A piece of text, picture or graphic which links a *Web page* to another Web page.

hypertext A word or group of words which are *hyperlinks*.

icon A small picture which you can click on to make your computer do something, or which shows you that your computer is doing something.

Information Superhighway Slang for the *Internet*.

intelligent agent (IA). A program which performs tasks on behalf of its user, and automatically adapts itself to its user's preferences.

Internet (or the Net). The worldwide computer *network* which is made up of many smaller networks.

Internet service providers (ISPs) also known as **Internet access providers** (IAPs) Companies that sell Net connections to people.

IP (Internet Protocol). The system used to specify how data is transferred over the *Internet*.

Java A programming language which works on all computers. It is used to add animations and interactive features to *Web pages*.

key word Any word that you ask a *search engine* to look for.

location box (or address box). The part of your *browser* where the *URLs* of *Web pages* are displayed.

log on/log in 1. Connect a computer to another computer. 2. Start up a computer.

menu A list of options from which a user selects.

modem (MOdulate/DEModulate). A device that allows computer data to be sent down an analog telephone line.

MUD (Multi-User Dungeon). A game which lots of people can play at the same time if they are all connected, via the *Net*, to a computer which is running the game.

Netiquette A code of conduct, developed by *Internet* users, which states acceptable and unacceptable ways of behaving on the *Net*.

Net surfer Someone who explores the *Net*, looking for interesting things to do.

Net surfing Exploring the *Net* by jumping from one file to another, like a surfer catching one wave and then another.

network A number of computers and other devices that are linked together so that they can share information and equipment.

off-line Not connected to the *Net*.

on-line Connected to the *Net*.

on-line service A company that gives you access to its private *network*, containing various kinds of information, as well as access to the *Internet*.

operator A word or symbol which gives a particular instruction to a *search engine*.

plug-in A piece of *software* you can add to your *browser* to enable it to perform extra functions, such as displaying video clips.

POP (Point of Presence). A point of access to the *Net*, usually a computer owned by an *Internet access provider*.

protocol An agreed set of rules that two computers use when communicating with each other.

public domain images Pictures that do not belong to a particular person or organization. You don't need to obtain permission to use these pictures.

query Instructions, made up of *key words* and *operators*, that you give to a *search engine* so it can find *Web pages* on a particular subject.

query box The place on a *search engine's home page* where you type your *query*.

register To type in details about yourself on a form on a *Web site* in order to gain access to the information on that site.

scanner A machine used to copy a picture or some text from paper onto a computer.

search engine (also known as a **search index**). A type of program which searches for *Web pages* which contain particular words.

serial port The part of a computer through which data can be transmitted. *Modems* are connected to computers through serial ports.

server A computer that carries out certain tasks for other computers on a *network*. Some servers store information that all the computers on the network use. Others link individual computers or small networks to big networks.

set-top box A piece of computer equipment that connects to your TV and lets you access the *Net*, or play computer games, using your TV as a screen.

shareware *Software* which you can try out before having to pay for it.

software Programs that enable computers to carry out certain tasks.

source code The *HTML code* that makes up a particular *Web page*.

subscribe Add your name to a list in order to access specific information. This may involve paying a fee.

tag An *HTML* instruction.

TCP/IP The language which allows your computer to join up to the *Internet*.

timeout When a computer gives up attempting a particular task because it has taken too long.

title The part of a *Web page* which appears in the title bar of your *browser* window.

trialware *Software* which you can try out for free before having to pay for it.

up A word used to describe a computer that is functioning.

upload To copy *files*, via the *Net*, from your computer to another computer.

URL (Uniform Resource Locator). The specific address of a resource on the *Internet*.

Virtual Reality (VR). The use of 3-D computer *graphics* to draw places and objects which you can move around.

virtual tourist Someone who uses the *Web* to visit museums and monuments in other places without leaving home.

virtual world A place created by a computer.

virus A program which interrupts the normal functioning of your *software* or *hardware*.

VRML (Virtual Reality Modeling Language). A programming language used to create *virtual worlds*.

Web master A person who creates or maintains a *Web site*.

Web page A computer document written in *HTML* and linked to other computer documents by *hyperlinks*.

Web site A collection of *Web pages* set up by an organization or an individual which are usually stored on the same *server*.

wired Connected to the *Net*.

World Wide Web A huge collection of information available on the Internet. The information is divided up into *Web pages* which are joined together by *hyperlinks*.

zip To make files smaller by compressing them.

Index

access providers, 9, 45
    cost, 42
    choosing, 42
    helpline, 9, 10, 42
addresses,
    e-mail, 25
    Web pages, 12, 43
advertisements, 33
applet, 29, 44
avatars, 39, 44

bandwidth, 40, 44
betaware, 27, 44
bits per second (bps), 7, 44
bookmarks, 16
browser, 8-9, 16, 44
    opening, 10-11
    personalizing, 30-31
    updating, 9
browsing (the Web), 14-15
bug, 44

cable modems, 40
cables, 40
cache, 31, 44
censorship software, 43
chat (3-D), 39
compressed files, 27
computer requirements, 6-7,
    38
connecting to the Internet,
    cost of, 42
    dial up, 9, 10, 42
    problems, 10
    software, 8-9
copyright, 16
costs,
    access providers, 42
    software, 27
crash, 15

dates,
    searching by, 22
default page, 11, 30
dial-up,
    connections, 9, 10, 44
    costs, 42
digital money, 33, 43, 44
Digital Video Discs, 41
directories, 18-19, 44
disconnecting (from the
    Net), 11
domain name, 12

Domain Name System, 44
downloading, 11, 44
    plug-ins, 29
    software, 26-27

e-mail, 25, 44
encryption, 33, 44
equipment, 6-7
error messages, 10

favorites, 16
freeware, 27, 44
FTP, 26, 44

games, 7, 28, 33
graphics card, 7

handshake, 10, 44
hardware, 6-7, 44
helper applications, 45
high-speed connections,
    40-41
hit, 20-21, 23, 45
home page (see also default
    page), 14, 45
host, 12, 45
hotlists, 16
HTML, 34-37, 45
HTTP, 12, 45
hyperlinks, 13, 14, 17, 18,
    19, 26, 31, 37, 45

icon, 11, 13, 14, 24, 45
Intelligent agents, 25, 45
Internet, 2, 45
    connecting to, 10-11
    providing access to, 42
    software, 8-9
Internet access providers,
    see access providers
Internet service providers,
    see access providers

Java, 29, 45

key words, 20-23, 45
Macintosh system, 6-7, 9,
Microsoft Internet Explorer,
    8, 10, 14-15, 16, 26, 30-31
Microsoft Windows, 9
modems, 6-7, 45
multimedia, 4, 6

Netscape Navigator, 8, 10-11,
    12, 14-15, 16, 26, 30-31
Net surfing, 15
Network Computers, 7, 45

off-line, 17, 31, 45
off-line viewing, 31
on-line, 2, 10, 30, 45
on-line malls, 32
on-line services, 42
operators, 21, 45
optimization, 9

passwords, 10, 24
personalizing,
    browser, 30-31
    search services, 24-25
personal pages, 5, 34-37
phrases,
    searching for, 22
pictures,
    including in Web pages, 36
    saving, 17
plug-ins, 28-29, 45
POP, 10, 42, 46
problems,
    connecting, 10
    with Virtual Reality, 41
protocol, 45, 46
protocol name, 12

RAM, 6, 29

safety, 43
satellites, 40
saving,
    links, 17
    pictures, 17
    plain text, 17
    Web pages, 17, 35
scanner, 36, 46
search engines, 20-23, 46
search results, 20, 23
search services, 18-23, 26, 43
    personalizing, 24-25
searching the Web, 18-23
    by date, 22
    by key word, 20-21
    for phrases, 22
servers, 12, 37, 46
shareware, 27, 43, 46
shopping, 32-33
sites, 14, 43

software, 46
    anti-virus, 43
    browser, 8-9
    censorship, 43
    cost of, 27
    decompressors, 27
    downloading, 26-27
    helper applications, 45
    Internet, 8-9
    sound card, 7
    streaming, 28
    subscription, 33, 46
    surfing, 15, 45

tags, 34-37
TCP/IP, 9, 46
telephone lines, 6, 9, 40
telephone networks, 6
timeout, 10, 46
trialware, 27, 46

updating (browsers), 9
uploading Web pages,
    37, 46
URLs, 12, 16, 26, 43, 46

video card, 7
Virtual Reality, 38-39, 41,
    46
virtual worlds, 38-39, 41,
    46
viruses, 43
VRML, 38-39

Web editors, 37
Web pages, 2, 4-5, 46
    addresses, 12, 43
    creating, 34-37
    downloading, 11
    finding, 18-23
    home pages, 14
    lists of, 43
    personal, 34-37
    saving, 17
    uploading, 37
Web radio, 28
Web sites, 14, 46
Web TV, 40
World Wide Web, 2, 46
    browsing, 14-15

zipped files, 27, 46

Every effort has been made to trace the copyright holders of the material in this book. If any rights have been omitted, the publishers offer their sincere apologies and will rectify this in any subsequent editions following notification.

  The material on Web sites changes from time to time. Usborne Publishing Ltd cannot be held responsible for the suitability of anything that may appear on the sites listed below.

Microsoft, Microsoft Windows, and Microsoft Internet Explorer are registered trademarks in the US and other countries. Screen shots and icons reprinted with permission from Microsoft Corporation.

Netscape and Netscape Navigator are registered trademarks of Netscape Communications Corporation in the US and other countries. Netscape's logos and Netscape product and service names are also trademarks of Netscape Communications Corporation, which may be registered in other countries.

Cover Globe. Space Frontiers Ltd./Planet Earth Pictures. Computer graphics. Telegraph Colour Library/V.C.L.
p4 Biker Mice from Mars. Copyright ©1997 Brentwood Television Funnies, Inc.
Star Wars. ™ & © Lucasfilm Ltd. (LFL) 1997. All Rights Reserved. COURTESY OF LUCAS FILM LTD. **www.starwars.com/**
Pie charts. Copyright ©1996 Tolga E. Yaveroglu.
Super Mario. Used with permission of THE Games.
MTV. With thanks to MTV Online.
Mona Lisa. © Louvre, Paris/ET Archive.
BMW. Copyright ©1997 BMW (GB) Ltd.
Spinning globe. ©Tony Stone Images.
p6 Multimedia PC supplied by Gateway 2000 Europe.
p7 Driving wheel supplied by Thrustmaster® Inc.
p13 With thanks to NASA.
p14 The LEGO illustrations are used with the permission of the LEGO group. **www.lego.com/**
p16 Cyber Tiger. Copyright ©1997 National Geographic Society. All rights reserved. **www.nationalgeographic.com/**
Young Composers graphic reprinted with permission from Mountain Lake Software, Inc. **www.youngcomposers.com/**
p17 GARFIELD © Paws, Inc. Dist by UNIVERSAL PRESS SYNDICATE. Reprinted with permission. All rights reserved.
p18 YAHOO! and the YAHOO! logo are trademarks of YAHOO!, Inc. Text and artwork copyright ©1996 by YAHOO! Inc. All rights reserved.
p19 With thanks to the National Museum of Natural History, Smithsonian Institution. **http://nmnhwww.si.edu/**
Natural History Museum screen. Copyright © The Natural History Museum, London. **www.nhm.ac.uk/**
p20 TEENAGE MUTANT NINJA TURTLES™ is a trademark owned and licensed by Mirage Studios. Used with permission.
Turtle Trax photograph. Copyright © Ursula Keuper Bennett and Peter Bennett. **www.turtles.org/**
Gulf of Maine Aquarium screen reproduced with permission of the Gulf of Maine Aquarium. **www.octopus.gma.org/**
Altavista. Copyright ©1997 Digital Equipment Corporation. All rights reserved.
p21 Bon Jovi. ©London Features International Ltd.
Spider. Nick Garbutt/Planet Earth Pictures.
P22 Leaning Tower of Pisa. Life File/Emma Lee.

Fashion pictures. With thanks to Benetton. **www.benetton.com/**
p23 WebCrawler and the WebCrawler logo are trademarks of Excite, Inc and may be registered in various jurisdictions. WebCrawler screen display copyright © 1995-1997 Excite, Inc. Toys'R'Us screen. Copyright © Geoffrey, Inc. **www.tru.com/**
p24 Sonic the Hedgehog © SEGA.
MY YAHOO! and the MY YAHOO! logo are trademarks of YAHOO!, Inc. Text and artwork copyright ©1996 by YAHOO! Inc. All rights reserved.
p28 Shockwave™ is a trademark of Macromedia®.
Yahtzee game used by permission of Andy Rogers.
QuickTime and the QuickTime logo are trademarks of Apple Computer, Inc., registered in the US and other countries and used with permission.
RealAudio and the RealAudio logo are registered trademarks of Progressive Networks, Inc. Copyright © Progressive Networks, Inc 1995-1997. All rights reserved.
Virgin Radio graphic. Copyright © Virgin Radio.
p29 CTW Online ©1997 Children's Television Workshop (CTW).
p30 Cyberkids graphic reprinted with permission from Mountain Lake Software, Inc. **www.cyberkids.com/**
p32 In-line skates. With thanks to Seneca Sports Inc.
T-shirt. Copyright © Hypno Design Inc. Used with permission.
Modern version of Machine Man, 4.75" tin toy wind up. Photo by John Eisner. ©1997 Rocket USA, Inc. **www.rocketusa.com/**
The original Machine Man was produced by Masudaya Corporation of Japan in the 1950s. **www.masudaya.com/**
VR dinner service. Copyright © The Virtual Reality Mall, Inc. Used with permission. All rights reserved.
Babylon 5. With thanks to Sonic Images. **www.sonicimages.com/**
p33 E-On is a registered trademark, and the E-On logo is a trademark of Entertainment Online Limited, reproduced with permission. Screens from the E-On Web site are copyright © 1997 Entertainment Online Limited. All rights reserved.
p36 Epson GT-9500 flatbed scanner. Used with permission.
p38 VR Piccadilly Circus as seen on Compuserve's VRcade shopping site. Used with permission.
VR space station. Copyright ©1997 Pixelwings, Wize and Dertschei.
AlphaWorld and Virtual Yellowstone screens from ActiveWorlds, **www.activeworlds.com/** Reproduced with permission of Circle of Fire Studios.
Avatars. With thanks to Onlive Technologies.
p40 IRIDIUM® satellite courtesy of Iridium LLC.
Motorola's CyberSURFR™ Cable Modem. Used by permission of Motorola.
Cables. Image Bank/Lars Ternblad.
p41 Jackson Square virtual world. Copyright © Planet 9 Studios. Jackson Square. Life File/Eddy Tan.
DVD drive. Used by permission of HITACHI EUROPE LTD.

First published in 1997 by Usborne Publishing, Ltd, Usborne House, 83-85 Saffron Hill, London EC1N 8RT, England. Copyright © 1997 Usborne Publishing Ltd. The name Usborne and the device ♛ are Trade Marks of Usborne Publishing Ltd. *All rights reserved.* No part of this publication may be reproduced, stored in a retrieval system or transmitted in any form or by any means, electronic, mechanical, photocopying, recording or otherwise, without the prior permission of the publisher. UE.
First published in America in March 1998.
Printed in Spain.